Sea Creatures

Sharks and Their Friends

Featuring DISNEY · PIXAR FINDING NEMO

Fish are friends, not food.

by David George Gordon

Sea Creatures is produced by becker&mayer!
Bellevue, Washington
www.beckermayer.com
Written by David George Gordon
Edited by Betsy Henry Pringle
Art direction and design by Lisa M. Douglass
Additional design assistance by Eunie Jung from Disney Press
Product development by Chris Tanner, Martin Meunier, and Christine Lee
Illustration assistance by Ryan Hobson
Production management by Jen Marx
Photographic research by Zena Chew
Facts checked by Arlo Moss and Melody Moss

Visit www.disneybooks.com
Printed in China
ISBN-13: 978-1-4231-0224-3
ISBN-10: 1-4231-0224-X
Library of Congress Cataloging-in-Publication Data on file
First Edition
1 2 3 4 5 6 7 8 9 10
06010

Let's See the Sea!

"If there is magic on this planet, it must be contained in water."
—Loren Eiseley, naturalist

Who doesn't enjoy spending time at the beach? Whether standing on the shore and letting the water gently tickle your toes or taking a swim or a boat ride, everyone has a favorite way to experience and enjoy the sea.

But did you ever stop to think about what goes on beneath the surface? The sea, which seems to have a life of its own, is actually home to millions of living creatures, from tiny plankton to enormous whales. Are you ready to dive in and meet some of the amazing animals that make their way through the wide watery world?

Come on, let's take the plunge!

Table of Contents

Sea Creatures

Some of the most beautiful and bizarre animals on Earth live in the world's oceans. At one time, sharks large enough to swallow an elephant ruled the seas. In today's watery realms, you'll discover fish that can inflate themselves like balloons, squid that are longer than the length of a house, and fish that thrive in water that is colder than ice cubes. All of these life-forms can be separated into two main groups: invertebrates (in-VER-tuh-braytz) and vertebrates (VER-tuh-braytz).

Fish are among the oldest forms of life on our planet.

Funny, I don't feel that old!

Jellyfish

Invertebrates

Invertebrate animals have no bones inside their bodies. Some have small spines in their skin or hard outer shells to give support to their otherwise soft flesh.

Types of Invertebrates

In the ocean, as well as on land, invertebrates greatly outnumber vertebrates. They account for 95 percent of all animal life on our planet. Invertebrate sea creatures include crabs, jellyfish, octopuses, sea stars, corals, and squid.

Fiddler Crab

Why are the oceans salty?

When rain falls, it hits mountaintops first and is then channeled into rivers. As the river water flows downhill, it picks up mineral salts from rocks and soil. The rivers eventually empty into the oceans and seas. When ocean water evaporates into the air or freezes into polar ice, the dissolved mineral salts are left behind, in the water that remains. Over time, this water gets saltier and saltier.

DISTILLED MOISTURE

SURFACE RUNOFF (EROSION)

SALT

RIVERBED

EVAPORATION

DISSOLVED SALTS (DO NOT EVAPORATE)

Vertebrates

Vertebrate animals have a skeleton inside their bodies. The skeleton has a spine, or backbone, and a skull to hold a brain. Some vertebrates who live in or depend upon the sea are: fish, marine mammals, sea turtles, and seabirds.

Fish

There are two types of fish: bony fish and cartilaginous (kar-te-LA-ge-nes) fish. Bony fish have hard, calcium-rich skeletons. Tuna, clown fish, sea horses, and salmon are examples of bony fish. Cartilaginous fish have incomplete skeletons made of cartilage, the same material that makes up the flexible part of your ears. Sharks, skates, and rays are cartilaginous fish.

Marine Mammals

Marine mammals have lungs instead of gills, and their bodies have hair, not scales. Whales, dolphins, and seals are marine mammals.

Sea Turtles

Sea turtles are born on land, but these long-distance swimmers quickly return to the sea. Leatherbacks and green sea turtles are examples of these creatures.

Seabirds

Seabirds live near the oceans and feast on fish and other sea creatures. Some seabirds can fly underwater, and others, like penguins, can't fly at all. Seagulls, terns, and pelicans are examples of seabirds.

Bony fish

Ray

Seals

Sea turtle

Seabird

What Makes a Fish a Fish

On the outside, being a fish is all about fins and scales. These body parts help the fish to move and protect itself from harm. On the inside, being a fish is about gills, cold blood, and an air-filled sac called a swim bladder. Without these features, fish couldn't survive underwater.

I may be cold—blooded, but I'm still a warm—hearted guy!

The dorsal fin gives the fish stability. On some fish, this fin runs the length of the animal's body.

By sweeping its twin-lobed caudal fin from side to side, the fish can move forward.

Like a ship's rudder, the paired pelvic fins help to steer the fish.

The anal fin lends stability and helps sweep away waste products.

Paired pectoral fins help the fish steer and stop abruptly.

Fins

Fins come in many shapes and sizes. A typical fish fin folds like a paper fan. The flesh on a fin is thin and floppy. Supports made of bone and cartilage make the fin rigid. Some fish fins, such as the pelvic and pectoral, are paired, just like human limbs. Others, such as the dorsal, anal, and caudal, are single fins. By fanning the water, fish use their fins to move straight ahead. By shifting the positions of their fins, the fish steer right, left, up, or down while they swim. Fins also help the fish stop suddenly or back up.

Scales

Scales cover the fish's body. Like small plates of armor, scales shield the fish from outside attackers, big and small.

One of the most common types of scale is called a *cycloid* scale. Cycloid scales overlap, much like the shingles on a house.

Many cartilaginous fish, including sharks, have tiny outgrowths called *denticles*. These are called *placoid* scales. The denticles make the shark's skin feel rough and abrasive. Long ago, carpenters used sharkskin instead of sandpaper to smooth wooden surfaces.

Placoid scales

Cycloid-scale growth rings

Cycloid scales

Juvenile fish have scales, but they may be difficult to see. As these fish grow, so do their scales. People can count the rings on cycloid scales, as they do with tree rings, to tell how old a fish may be.

Gills

Gills help fish breathe. Gills are feathery structures that capture and remove oxygen molecules in the water. They also release molecules of carbon dioxide—the waste product of respiration—from the fish's bloodstream.

As a fish's mouth opens and closes, it pumps water over the gills and out through an opening behind the head. A flap protects this opening. Sharks don't have this bony flap, called the *operculum*, so their gill slits are visible.

Gills

Cold Blood

A fish's insides are similar to your own. Gills take the place of lungs in a fish's body. But other than that, a fish has a heart, brain, stomach, intestines, and reproductive organs, just like you do. There's even a kidney—just one, not two—that runs along the fish's back.

There's one big difference, though, between humans and fish: humans and other mammals are warm-blooded. This means they can control their body temperature, holding their inner heat at an even 98.6 degrees Fahrenheit at all times. Fish can't do that: they are cold-blooded. Their body temperatures rise and fall, depending on the temperature of their watery surroundings.

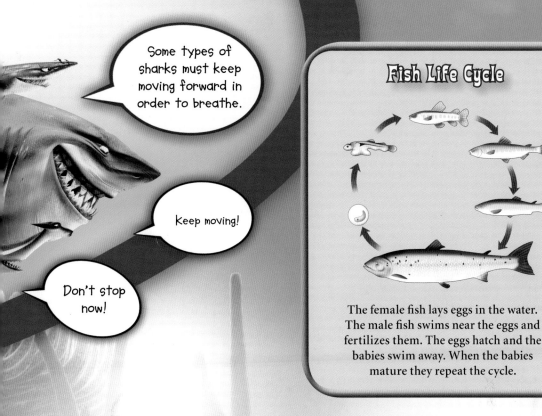

Some types of sharks must keep moving forward in order to breathe.

Keep moving!

Don't stop now!

Fish Life Cycle

The female fish lays eggs in the water. The male fish swims near the eggs and fertilizes them. The eggs hatch and the babies swim away. When the babies mature they repeat the cycle.

How Fish Float

A fish's swim bladder helps it stay afloat. This special organ works like an inflatable beach toy. By adjusting the amount of gas in the swim bladder, the fish makes itself more or less buoyant. When the bladder is full, the fish floats upward. When it empties, the fish drifts downward. It's as simple as that.

Instead of swim bladders, sharks rely on an enormous oil-filled liver to stay buoyant. Because oil is lighter than water, the liver balances this fish's heavy bulk.

Shark liver

FACT ATTACK!

Fossil fish bones and scales have been discovered in rocks that are 400 million years old. The Devonian period, about 350 million years ago, has been called the Age of Fishes, because fish were so plentiful way back then.

Ocean Habitats

Oceans cover nearly three-fourths of the planet's surface. Life began in the water and, today, eighty percent of all life on Earth is found in the oceans. The oceans can support many different kinds of life because oceans themselves have so many different environments. Differences in water temperature, pressure, amount of light, and abundance of food enable an amazing diversity of creatures to make their homes in this watery wonderland.

SHORE		LIGHT PENETRATION	Ocean Zones	
NEARSHORE				
			SUNLIT ZONE	200 Meters
			TWILIGHT ZONE	1,000 Meters
			THE ABYSS	6,000 Meters

Shore

Mudflats, sandy beaches, and rocky shores—these places serve as transition zones between land and water. When the tide rises or strong winds push ocean waves ashore, the lines between these habitats become blurred. During these times, these "edgy" environments are temporarily covered by seawater. Sometimes that water is captured in small pits or depressions in the rocks, creating what are commonly called *tide pools*—natural outdoor aquariums filled with animals and plants.

Nearshore

A bit farther out to sea is a region known as the *nearshore*. The water here is shallow, and the bottom may be covered by plants or strewn with rocks. Many marine animals benefit from the comparatively calm seas and mild weather that come with closer proximity to a protective coast. Food is plentiful, often carried by freshwater rivers and streams that flow into the sea.

Let's name the zones of the open sea!

Sunlit Zone

Beyond the nearshore is the open ocean. In this domain, life is abundant from the surface down to about 650 feet (200 meters). We call this layer the *sunlit zone*. Tiny plants and animals abound in the sunlit zone, and these morsels feed larger creatures. In turn, even larger animals, such as squid, crabs, fish, sea turtles, and great white sharks, eat the bigger life-forms.

The expanses of the open ocean may be broken by undersea ridges or mountain ranges rising up from the seafloor. When the tips of those ridges and ranges break the surface, they create islands. In tropical seas, islands are often fringed by complex, well-populated underwater communities called *coral reefs*.

Twilight Zone

Below the sunlit zone is the *twilight zone*. This zone extends to 3,300 feet (1,000 meters). The animals that dwell here must be able to withstand tremendous pressure and near-freezing temperatures.

The Abyss

Below the twilight zone is the black *abyss*. In these icy depths, where the sun has never shone, the only light comes from eerie glow-in-the-dark fish.

Life in a Tide Pool

Want to get up close and personal with some fish and other sea life? Then come to the rocky seashore at low tide. At least once a day—and, in some parts of the world, twice a day—the ocean recedes, revealing small "natural aquariums" filled with fish and other sea life. Hours later, the waves return, and the tide pools are again covered by seawater. Then the cycle repeats itself.

Sculpin

Find the Fish

The mottled colors of the tide pool sculpin help it to blend in with the pink, purple, and gray hues of its rocky surroundings. The sculpin is most at home hiding in its tide pool. If a strong wave washes this small fish from its lair, the sculpin relies on a keen sense of smell to guide itself back in.

Anemones

Sea anemones (uh-NEH-muh-neez) look like flowers, but they are stationary invertebrates that attach themselves to hard surfaces. These distant relatives of jellyfish trap prey with their stinging tentacles. If attacked, they can uproot themselves and move to a new location. Giant green anemones get their bright hues from microscopic algae growing in their guts.

Anemone

Shell Game

It looks like an empty shell . . . but it's not! To protect itself from predators, the hermit crab hides in an empty snail shell. It hangs on with its hind legs and, when threatened, quickly ducks deep inside the shell. Eventually, the hermit crab will outgrow the snail shell. When that happens, it will move into a bigger one. If necessary, it will even steal a better shell from another hermit crab. Why do hermit crabs play this shell game? This crab doesn't have a hard shell, so it uses shells from other animals for protection.

Hermit crab

Cling fish

And I thought I'd seen some strange things in Dr. Sherman's office!

Hanging On

Northern cling fish are well named. They use their fins like suction cups to attach themselves firmly to the undersides of rocks in a tide pool. Try as you might, you won't separate this persistent fish from its rocky surface. When the tide returns, the cling fish will choose to return to the sea on its own.

Ammonite fossil

FACT ATTACK!

In the days before and during the age of the dinosaurs, animals known as *ammonites* populated the seas. Ammonites were probably one of the most dominant forms of life 400 million years ago. Many ammonites were small, but some grew to be as large as 6.5 feet (2 meters) long.

Coral Reef Cities

Coral reefs are the most diverse and action-packed underwater environments on the planet. All the hustling, bustling fish make this habitat seem like a city beneath the sea. This underwater city gets its structure from the maze of living columns and clusters known as *corals*. Each coral structure contains hundreds—and in the larger forms, millions—of small, soft-bodied animals called *polyps*. The polyps secrete calcium carbonate—the same rugged material that seashells are made of. When the calcium hardens, it forms the coral's rock-hard skeleton, giving structure to the reef.

Sea fan

Sea Fans

Thousands of polyps cooperate to form sea fans—brightly colored animals whose branches make them look like plants. The polyps grab bits of food carried by water currents that flow through the fan. The polyps usually stay out of sight during the day and work at night, when most polyp-eating fish are sleeping.

Menacing Mouth

That mouthful of curved, daggerlike teeth makes a moray eel look mean. This animal is fairly mellow, though, unless it's hungry and you happen to be a fish, lobster, or crab. Morays must keep their mouths open wide to breathe. There are 200 kinds of morays, mostly in tropical seas.

Moray eel

Flame angelfish

Clown Fish Assembly

1. Find the organs marked CF. Press the two holes on the organs onto the two pegs inside the clown fish body.
2. Press the spine onto the peg and the hole inside the body.
3. Insert the display pole on the stand into the hole on the fish model.

When two species help each other it's called mutualism. In other words, everybody wins!

Fiery Fish

It's easy to see how the flame angelfish got its name. Those blazing orange and red hues on its body may serve as a warning to other fish. Despite its small size, about 4 inches (10 cm) in length, this fish is as feisty as it is fiery. "Stand back! This chunk of coral belongs to me!" the flame angelfish seems to say.

Happy Together

Ordinarily, sea anemones capture and feed on fish. However, percula clown fish have a special mucus layer that protects them from the anemones' stinging tentacles. The clown fish swim among the anemones, feeding on tidbits the anemones have left behind from previous hunting trips. As a trade-off, the clown fish chase away anemone-eating predators.

15

Down on the Sandy Seafloor

At first glance, the sandy seafloor appears to be a lifeless desert. On closer inspection, it becomes a bountiful environment, rich with sea life.

Eelgrass

On sunny summer days, the shallow water near the shore is warm and the sand is smooth. But when fierce winter storms roll in, crashing waves and whirlwinds of sand create dangerous conditions for the sea creatures that make their homes here. By burrowing into the sand, these creatures protect themselves from bad weather and hungry predators.

Undersea Grasslands

Those long-waving blades belong to eelgrass plants. They form welcoming beds for fringe-dwelling fish and other creatures. Small fish like to play hide-and-seek among the blades, avoiding bigger predators while hunting for morsels to eat. Eelgrass beds are important spawning sites for silvery schools of surf smelt and sand lance. Known as forage fish or baitfish, the smelt and sand lance serve as food for seabirds and bigger fish.

Buried by Beach Sand

A patch of sand suddenly comes alive. It's a juvenile bat ray, a common inhabitant of deep water, coming closer to shore to forage for food. To avoid becoming a meal for other seashore animals, the ray conceals itself under a light dusting of beach sand. This fish might look scary, but it's usually harmless to humans.

Bat ray

> I'll have the shrimp and eelgrass salad.... All right, hold the shrimp!

> There's nothing fishy about you, mate! It's just eelgrass for me, too!

Goby and Shrimp

Burrowing Roommates

Sometimes, creatures share the same underwater burrow and help each other out. Blind shrimp and small fish called yellow watchman gobies are two such roommates. The tiny goby can't dig, and the shrimp can't see predators. So, the goby stands guard while the shrimp, with one antenna always touching the fish, digs a burrow. If a predator comes near, the goby wiggles its tail to alert the blind shrimp, and both roommates duck into the hole for cover.

Too Big for Its Britches?

Geoducks

The geoduck (GOO-ee-duck) clam digs deep into the sand. To breathe while buried, it stretches its three-foot-long (1 meter) neck upward to reach the surface of the seafloor. It draws water through this siphon, and gills remove the dissolved oxygen the clam needs to breathe. The gills also strain out the small marine plants that the geoduck feeds on. Snug in the sand and mud, a geoduck can live for 150 years and weigh 20 pounds (9 kg). The geoduck's body is so plump that it can't close its shell.

Swimming in the Open Sea

The majority of marine animals, including most fish, spend their lives far from shore—feeding, breeding, and cavorting in the vast, unbroken expanses of the ocean. In the open sea, waves can be 50 to 100 feet high. In addition, water is about 750 times denser than air. For these reasons, many of the animals who live here have muscular bodies with streamlined shapes.

Sunfish

The ocean sunfish is the world's heaviest bony fish. Adults can weigh up to 2.5 tons (2.3 metric tons). These deep-sea fish appear to be little more than a head with fins. To get around, they flap their large dorsal and anal fins from side to side while using the tail as a rudder for steering.

Sunfish

Long-Distance Travelers

Salmon make seasonal journeys between breeding and feeding grounds that are thousands of miles apart. A young salmon's trail might begin at the mouth of a coastal stream in Washington or Oregon. Once the fish leaves these calm waters, it heads west, following ocean currents to reach destinations as distant as Japan. When nature signals that it is time to reproduce, the salmon somehow finds its way back to the very stream of its birth. Scientists think that salmon are guided by scents in the water and many other subtle clues.

Salmon

Sea Turtle Assembly

1. Find the organs marked ST. Fit together the hole on the organs and the peg inside the top shell. Press the two pieces together.

2. Press the two pegs on the bottom shell into the two holes on the bottom of the top shell.

Green sea turtle

Green Sea Turtles

Green sea turtles get their name from the green-colored fat that helps to insulate their bodies. These streamlined swimmers with large front flippers live mainly close to the shore. When it is time to nest, green turtles will migrate more than 1,200 miles (2,000 km) to reach their breeding site.

FACT ATTACK!

Schools containing hundreds of thousands of salmon, herring, or cod race through the open ocean, feeding on small fish and invertebrates. How do they keep from bumping into each other or colliding with objects in their paths? Most fish have a secret sense, called the *lateral line*. This sense allows them to feel slight changes in water pressure and currents caused by other fish or objects nearby. Having this information allows the fish to swim in close formation and avoid obstacles, even while swimming at high speeds.

Fish school

19

Life Without Sunlight

A mile below the surface of the ocean, there's no sunlight to help plants grow. The temperature is 30 degrees Fahrenheit—two degrees below the normal freezing point of water. The pressure is extreme—over two tons per square inch (1.8 metric tons/6.4 square centimeters)—yet somehow, sea creatures manage to survive and even thrive at these depths.

Challenger Deep in the western Pacific is the deepest point of the oceans. If the base of Mount Everest were at the bottom of the trench, the peak of the mountain would be 6,770 feet (2,000 meters) below sea level! Even at this depth, tiny sea creatures, called forams, have been found.

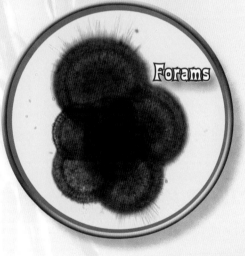

Forams

Cardinal fish

3-D View

The cardinal fish's huge eyes are ideal for peering into the darkness of extreme depths. Because they capture even the faintest light rays, those big eyes are a real benefit down here. But there's another reason why these fish get along so well. The cardinal's big, bulgy eyes provide overlapping fields of vision.

Viper Fish

The deeper we go, the stranger the sea life seems. The viper fish has huge fangs that slant backward, coming dangerously close to the fish's large eyes. This monstrous-looking animal also sports a flashing light on its top fin. The dot acts like a fishing lure, drawing other deep-sea denizens near.

Viper fish

Fishing Fish

Anglerfish

The deep-sea anglerfish has a face that only its mother could love. Its eyes are tiny, its mouth is enormous, and its fins are short and stumpy—perfect for hopping around like a toad on the seafloor. To attract other fish, it waves a glow-in-the-dark lure that resembles a worm. This "fishing pole" is a specialized fin that contains millions of light-producing bacteria. The bacteria generate light through a chemical reaction. This phenomenon is called *bioluminescence* (BI-oh-LUME-en-ES-ense)— a word that literally means "living light."

Gulper Eel

The gulper eel opens its loosely hinged jaws and balloons out its mouth to capture other deep-sea fish. Prey is caught in the animal's pouchlike lower jaw. It's from this pouch that the fish gets its other common name—the umbrella-mouth gulper. Specimens as long as six feet (1.8 meters) have been caught in all the world's oceans, usually at depths ranging from 3,000 to 6,000 feet (1–2 km). The gulper's tail is tipped with a glow-in-the-dark organ that probably attracts light-seeking fish and invertebrates.

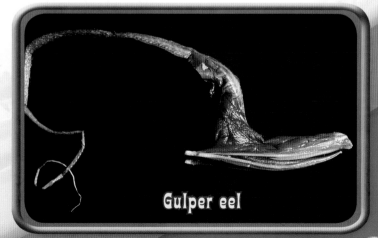

Gulper eel

Survival at Sea

In a fish-eat-fish world, it's best to be prepared. Many forms of sea life rely on dirty tricks to gain the advantage over their neighbors. Knives, poison, spikes—if it guarantees survival in this cutthroat environment, it's a good thing.

Lionfish

Venom

Look, but don't touch! The sharp spines in a lionfish's long frilly fins are tipped with paralyzing venom. This keeps bigger predatory fish from getting too close. While hunting, lionfish spread their long fins and use them to herd prey into a corner. A quick snap of the jaws and it's all over for the cornered fish, shrimp, or crab.

So people want to come here, but they don't want us to show them our best smiles? That's downright unfriendly!

FACT ATTACK!

The Moses sole, a resident of the Red Sea, secretes foul-tasting chemicals when sharks attack. Since this works for the sole, why not try it for people? Scientists are studying ways to turn this bitter toxin, called *pardaxin*, into a natural shark repellent.

Stonefish

Stinging Stonefish

This warty-looking relative of the lionfish is perhaps the deadliest creature in the sea. Called a stonefish, this reef fish is armed with thirteen stout spines in the dorsal fin. Each spine can inject highly toxic venom that causes intense pain. Lucky for us, a medicine has been invented to combat the effect of the stonefish's venom.

The Cutting Edge

They don't call them surgeonfish for nothing. On either side of its body, near the base of the tail, the blue surgeonfish has a sharp scale that it wields like a surgeon's scalpel. Anyone foolish enough to fiddle with this fish might get some on-the-spot surgery. When not in use, the scalpel-like scale folds into a slot on the fish's body.

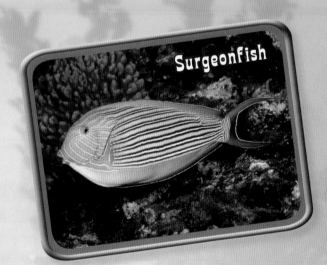
Surgeonfish

Zapped!

Specialized organs in the torpedo ray's muscles can generate powerful electric shocks—up to 220 volts—to stun prey or scare away predators. The ray produces both high- and low-voltage shocks for these two purposes.

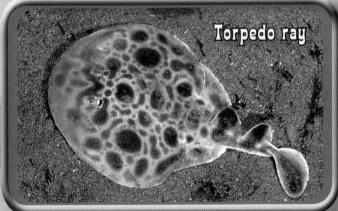
Torpedo ray

Color and Camouflage

Many fish communicate with color. You can learn plenty about these animals if you can read what their bright colors, bold stripes, and detailed patterns are telling you.

The color patterns, hues, and body shapes of some fish are designed to blend in with their surroundings. They may be lying in wait before popping out of a hiding place and nabbing the "catch of the day." Or they may use their protective colors to hide from other predators.

Female wrasse

Male wrasse

Quick-Change Artists

Female rainbow wrasses have body stripes of red, yellow, and black. The males have blue heads, purple bodies, and a yellow band between the two colors. Unbelievably, a female rainbow wrasse can change sexes and become a male. When this happens, the fish changes colors, too.

Juvenile emperor angelfish are bluish black with alternating light blue and white circles on their bodies. Adults have yellow-and-blue bodies, white faces, and black masks. If you didn't know better, you'd think the two were unrelated.

Look THAT Way!

Longnose butterfly fish wear dark masks that hide their eyes. Near the tail, these reef fish have a black blotch that resembles an eye. These markings make it look like the fish is facing in the opposite direction. Most predators can't tell which end is which. This misdirection allows the longnose butterfly fish to dodge danger.

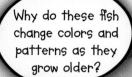

Why do these fish change colors and patterns as they grow older?

Only the angelfish knows for sure.

Butterfly fish

Adult and baby angelfish

Flatfish

Master of Disguise

Flatfish are true masters of disguise. They can turn on special pigment cells in their skin to match the patterns and colors of the sand or gravel they lie upon. Since most flatfish have no other form of protection against predators, camouflage means the difference between life and death for them.

Hidden from Above and Below

Probably the most popular form of camouflage among fish is called *countershading*. You can see it in the dark back and white belly of a blue shark. When viewed from above the water, the dark-colored back helps the shark blend in with the dark bottom below it. When viewed from below, the shark's white belly helps it blend in with the bright sky above it.

Invertebrates

Fish share their waters with all kinds of invertebrate companions. Two of these, *cnidarians* and *echinoderms*, are some of the most bizarre animals on Earth.

> Look, but don't touch, dude—they may look like softies, but jellyfish can sting something fierce.

Coral

Cnidarians

Cnidarians (nye-DARE-ee-enz) are radially symmetrical. That is, their body parts spread outward from a central hub, much like the spokes on a wheel. Cnidarians have stinging cells, called *nematocysts* (nuh-MAT-o-sists), which they use like harpoons to snag prey. Familiar cnidarians are corals and sea jellies.

Lion's mane jellyfish

Giant Jellyfish

The arctic lion's mane jellyfish is a giant among sea jellies. Its body, or "bell," can be seven feet (2 meters) across and its long, dangling tentacles have been measured at over 120 feet (36.5 meters). You'd think a creature this size could eat whatever it wanted, but this cold-water invertebrate feeds solely on plankton, tiny fish, and smaller-sized jellies. Like all sea jellies, the lion's mane has no heart and no brain.

Echinoderms

Like cnidarians, spiny-skinned echinoderms (e-KI-nuh-dermz) are radially symmetrical. But unlike any other animal, their bodies are based on the number five. Examples of echinoderms are sea stars (starfish), sea urchins, sand dollars, and sea cucumbers.

Giant sea star

Sand Dollar

Those hard white disks you see on the beach are the bleached skeletons of sand dollars. Live sand dollars are brown and fuzzy and live on the sandy seafloor. These flat, hard-skinned relatives of sea stars are covered with tiny hairs. Sand dollars feed on microscopic morsels of food in the sand. The tiny hairs help move the food particles to the sand dollar's mouth.

Sand dollars

Sea Star

Most people call them starfish, but the 2,000 varieties of sea stars are invertebrates, not fish. Sea stars have hundreds of tube feet on each of their five arms. They use these feet to pry open clamshells. To eat, the sea star's stomach pops out of its mouth and slides into the clamshell. After it digests the clam, the stomach slides back into the sea star. If a sea star loses an arm, it can slowly grow it back. And some types of sea stars can grow an entirely new body from one severed arm!

Chocolate chip sea star

A chocolate chip sea star? Sounds totally tasty, doesn't it? Forget it, though. Its outsides are wicked tough.

The word *cephalopod* means, basically, that the animal's legs come out of its head.

Cephalopods

What has eight arms, a parrot's beak, and green blood? No, it's not a monster from outer space. It's an octopus—one member of a class of animals called *cephalopods* (SE-fel-le-podz). Traits shared by cephalopods include well-developed heads, many flexible arms or tentacles, and, in most cases, a nearly invisible shell. Many cephalopods have suckers on their arms to catch prey.

Octopus

Squid

Underwater Einsteins

Cephalopods belong to a larger group of animals called *mollusks*. These include oysters, clams, snails, slugs, and many other soft-bodied creatures. The cephalopods are believed to be the brains of this bunch. In laboratories, octopuses quickly learn how to scramble through mazes and can be taught to distinguish squares, circles, and triangles lowered into their tanks. Scientists have shown that octopuses can play games and also unscrew the lids of jars to get to the food inside.

Jet Propelled

Squid and their relatives rely on a kind of "jet propulsion" to get around. By squirting water backward through a tube-shaped opening called a siphon, the streamlined squid scoots like a jet through the sea. For the squid, speed counts. There are many faster animals eager to sample these fleeting morsels. Some squid have both sharp hooks and suckers on their arms. These help them capture and hold prey.

Mimic octopus "sea star"

Marine Mimic

The Indonesian mimic octopus contorts its body and changes color to impersonate other sea creatures. If aggressive tropical damselfish bother the octopus, it will cramp six of its legs down a burrow and then spread the other two to resemble a sea snake, which preys on these fish. To swim above the seafloor, the octopus will extend its brown-and-white-striped arms to look like a deadly lionfish. This octo-impersonator can mimic at least eight venomous creatures, including rays, sponges, and flounders.

Mimic octopus "flounder"

A Living Fossil

The basic body plan of the chambered nautilus has changed very little in 150 million years. This animal lives in the deep waters of the tropical Pacific Ocean. By adjusting the amount of fluid in its many-chambered shell, it moves upward and downward, much like a hot-air balloon. This animal has more than 90 tentacles, which it uses to taste and touch its favorite food—shrimp.

Nautilus

Crustaceans

What do crustaceans, such as crabs, shrimp, and lobsters, have in common with grasshoppers, spiders, and ants? They're all *arthropods*—animals with jointed limbs. These creatures are wrapped in thick body armor, much like a medieval knight. This armor has flexible joints so the creature can bend at the knee and elbow. Crustaceans have two pairs of antennae, five pairs of legs, and fan-shaped tails. With over 50,000 known species, they are some of the most abundant forms of life in the sea.

Spider crab

Crabs—Big and Small

Crabs come in all shapes and sizes. The largest is the Japanese giant crab, with outstretched claws that can measure 13 feet (4 meters) from tip to tip. This enormous crustacean would cast a long shadow over the European long-beaked spider crab, which, at its biggest, is barely half an inch (1.2 cm) in diameter. Even though walking sideways is called a "crab walk," crabs are able to walk in any direction.

Dungeness Crab

Eight-inch-wide (20 cm) Dungeness crabs live in eelgrass beds near the shores of the western United States. Because

Dungeness crab

their hard shells keep them from growing, about once a year the shell splits open and the crab crawls out. Without its shell, the crab's body is soft and unprotected. The animal goes through a growth spurt. In a few days, the new shell hardens, stopping the crab's growth for another year. This process is called *molting*.

Snapping shrimp

Noisy Shrimp

Snapping shrimp have a special claw that creates a loud snapping sound. The snap creates a powerful water jet that can stun small fish five feet (1.5 meters) away. The shrimp live in large colonies under the waves. These colonies are so noisy that submarines can use them to hide from enemy ships' sound-seeking sonar.

Filling up on Krill

Some of the biggest sea creatures chow down on the smallest ones. Many kinds of large fish and whales fill their bellies with krill. These tiny relatives of prawns and shrimp feed on still smaller animals, including microscopic crustaceans called copepods. Krill live in all the world's oceans.

At Your Service

Banded coral shrimp are also called cleaner shrimp because of the special service they provide. These bright red-and-white crustaceans set up cleaning stations on coral reefs. Fish come to these locales to have the shrimp pick parasites from their bodies. The fish will even let the cleaner shrimp inspect the insides of their mouths. Somehow, the fish understand that these shrimp are too valuable to be made into snacks.

Coral shrimp

Crab Assembly

1. Gently pry off the top shell with your fingernail.
2. Place the green organs inside the body.
3. Press the two pegs on the top shell into the holes on the body.

Sharks, Skates, and Rays

Sharks, skates, and rays are some of the oldest fish in the sea. The ancestors of these animals shared the ocean with aquatic dinosaurs and life-forms considerably more ancient than that. In all that time, the basic body plans of these cartilaginous fish have changed very little.

Hammerhead shark

Great white shark

Manta ray

Great Whites

The great white is a magnificent creature, with dozens of razor-sharp teeth packed in its powerful jaws. Great whites, which can be over twenty feet long (6 meters) and weigh more than two tons (1.8 metric tons), are powerful enough to jump completely out of the water. Although these animals have a reputation for being "man-eaters," great white sharks are better described as "man-biters." In more than half of all known great white shark attacks on swimmers, the attackers took only one bite and then swam away.

Underwater Wings

The enlarged pectoral fins of skates and rays form "wings" that undulate gracefully as they glide through the water. Some of these flat-bodied fish, like the manta ray, reach enormous proportions. Newborn mantas are about four feet (1.2 meters) across, and adults can have a wingspan of 25 to 30 feet (7.6 to 9 meters). That's large enough for the ray to give a scuba diver a free ride.

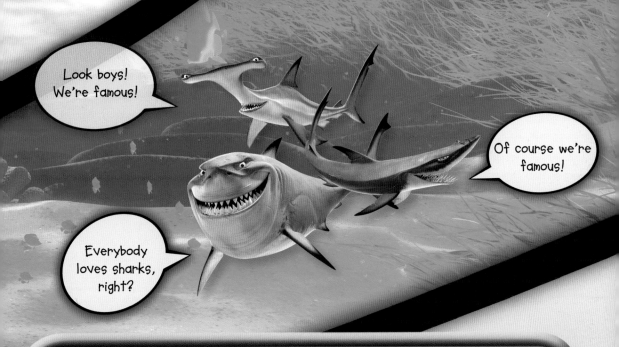

Shark Assembly

1. Fit the pectoral fin onto the body.
2. Press the two pegs on the skeleton into the two holes inside the body.
3. Slide the organs marked GWS a little bit inside the gill arches and then press the hole in the organs onto the peg inside the body.
4. Attach the left pectoral fin.

Hammerheads

The eyes of a hammerhead shark are set far apart, at the ends of the fish's long, T-shaped head. As it swims, the hammerhead shark slowly swings its head from side to side to get a panoramic view of its surroundings. The odd-shaped head also acts as a stabilizer, improving the shark's swimming abilities.

FACT ATTACK!

The largest fossil shark is called Megalodon. Its name means "big teeth." When alive, Megalodon could open its mouth wide enough to swallow an elephant-size animal in one bite!

Marine Mammals

Like people, marine mammals are warm-blooded; they have lungs; their bodies have hair (not scales); and they nurse their babies with milk from paired mammary glands. Unlike people, marine mammals spend all or most of their lives in the water. Marine mammals are some of the largest and smartest animals ever to exist.

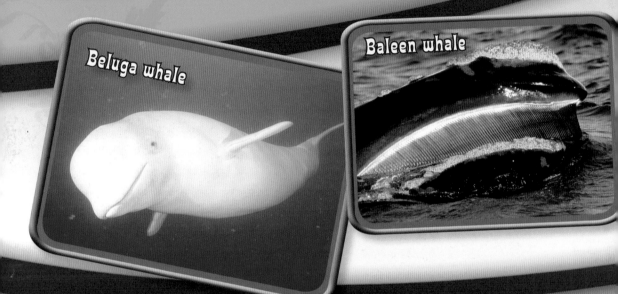

Beluga whale

Baleen whale

Whales

Whales are huge, streamlined, aquatic animals with large brains. Whales travel in groups called pods. All whales breathe air into their lungs through blowholes at the top of their enormous heads. When whales reach the surface of the water to breathe, they forcefully blow air out through the blowhole.

Some whales have teeth. Toothed whales eat fish, squid, and other marine mammals. Toothed whales have only one blowhole. The largest whales have comblike filters in their mouths called *baleen*. As the whales scoop or gulp water filled with plankton, krill, and small fish, the baleen acts like a strainer, holding onto the nourishing food while allowing the water to run out. Baleen whales have two blowholes.

A Whale Serenade

Long ago, sailors called beluga whales "sea canaries." That's because these all-white whales make eerie whistling sounds. Some people believe the beluga's vocalizations may have inspired shipboard legends about sweet-singing mermaids.

Sperm whale

Narwhal

Fish Story

Sixty-foot-long (18 meters) sperm whales are believed to be the largest toothed animals on earth. Sperm whales are able to dive to the ocean's depths, making them one of the only animals that can feast on giant squid. They were once hunted for their layer of body fat, or blubber. The whales would struggle to escape the whalers' harpoons, sometimes overturning whaling boats with their tails, or crashing headfirst into ships. *Moby Dick*, a story about a rare all-white whale, may have been based on an encounter with an actual albino sperm whale.

Unicorn or Whale?

In eleventh-century Europe, some people believed in the unicorn—a mythical animal with a long spiraling horn on its forehead. The myth was kept alive by the Vikings, who sometimes returned from ocean voyages carrying similar-shaped horns. We now know that those horns came from the narwhal, a small arctic whale with a single twisted tusk.

More Marine Mammals

Whales aren't the only warm-blooded animals in the sea. They share their favorite swimming holes with a host of closely related sea mammals, such as porpoises, dolphins, sea lions, and seals. All of these animals eat fish and shellfish.

Dolphin

Elephant seal

Sea lion

Deep-Sea Divers

Seals and sea lions are world-champion free divers. The deepest diver is the northern elephant seal, which often descends to a depth of 4,000 feet (1.2 km). It can hold its breath for more than an hour—about 60 times the depth and duration of the average human swimmer. Male elephant seals, called bulls, have a huge nose that resembles an elephant's trunk.

Dolphins to the Rescue

Dolphins are natural enemies of sharks. Mothers protect their calves by rushing at sharks and battering them with their bodies. Dolphins have also been known to rescue swimmers from shark attacks. In ancient Greece, dolphins were said to save shipwrecked sailors from drowning. In modern-day southern Brazil, dolphins have been helping to chase fish into fishermen's nets. Town records show that this sort of teamwork has been taking place for at least 150 years!

Orca

When orcas raise their heads out of the water, that's called spy hopping.

Orca Assembly

1. Press the peg on the pectoral fin into the hole on the orca's body.
2. Fit the tail onto the body.
3. Press the peg on the spine and the hole in the skull into the body.
4. Press the organs marked O onto the peg inside the body.
5. Press the rib cage with the pectoral fin onto the pegs on the spine.

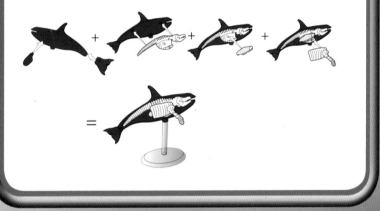

Echolocation

Bottlenose dolphins and others of their kind use sound to "see" underwater. They make noises and then listen to the sound as it bounces off objects around them. The returning sound waves help them navigate and find food without colliding with rocks, pilings, or other dolphins in their path. This is called *echolocation*. Some species produce extraloud sounds to stun nearby fish or squid. The dolphins then swing around and gobble up the sound-stunned prey.

Orcas

Orcas, or killer whales, are the largest dolphins in the world. An adult can be about 32 feet (9.7 meters) long. Found in all the world's oceans, these handsome black-and-white predators live in stable family units and communicate with one another with a language of clicks and whistles. The dorsal fin of a full-grown male orca may tower six feet (1.8 meters) over its back. Whale researchers use the shape of the dorsal fin and the distinctive gray "saddle patch" on an orca's back to recognize individuals in a group.

Sea Turtles and Seabirds

The ocean's abundance of life fuels two unusual and quite unexpected forms of life—sea turtles and seabirds. Over eons, both have found ways of living comfortably in, on, or above the waves.

Sea Turtles

Although relatives of these large seagoing reptiles were swimming in the oceans long before the age of dinosaurs, sea turtles are now endangered by pollution and fishing nets.

Unlike people, who breathe heavily while exercising, sea turtles rely on the air stored in their large, elastic lungs. When their blood oxygen levels become extralow, the turtles rise from the depths and raise their heads above water, breathing deeply at the surface. With their lungs refilled, the sea turtles dive again. The air in their lungs can sustain these flipper-powered sojourners to depths of 500 feet (152 meters).

Baby sea turtle

Life Cycle

When sea turtles are between 20 and 50 years old, they migrate from their open-sea feeding grounds to a nesting beach in order to mate. After mating, the females dig holes on the beach to bury their leathery-shelled eggs. Over a period of weeks, the females lay as many as 120 eggs in each hole. Then the females return to the sea. When the eggs hatch about 7–12 weeks later, the baby sea turtles return to the sea, and the cycle starts again.

Large Leatherbacks

The leatherback is the largest living sea turtle, averaging six feet (1.8 meters) in length with a weight of 1,400 pounds (635 kg). Instead of a hard shell of scales, this turtle has a leathery back with raised gray stripes. Dug into the beach sand, a single leatherback nest may contain as many as 80 eggs.

Leatherback sea turtle

World-Class Traveler

Each year, the arctic tern migrates from the northeast tip of the United States and Canada to Antarctica and back again. In the process, this lightweight bird covers well over 20,000 miles (32,186 km)—the greatest distance to be covered by a single animal. How they remember the route is a great mystery to scientists.

Arctic tern

Penguins

Penguins use their flipperlike wings to whip around underwater and leap from the water like dolphins. These flightless black-and-white birds live only in the southern hemisphere, where they spend 75 percent of their time in the water.

Penguin

Pelican Pouches

Pelican

Brown pelicans have enormous bills that can hold nearly three times their stomach capacity! This amazing pouch also helps keep pelicans cool on hot days. By fluttering its pouch, the pelican brings its warm blood in close contact with the outside air, much like an elephant flapping its big ears.

Who's the Biggest?

The size of land-dwelling animals is limited by the downward pull of gravity. That is, these creatures can only grow so large before the weight of their own bodies sends them crashing to the ground. Aquatic animals have no such limits to size. With water to support all that weight, they can grow as big as they please.

Blue whale

A Whopping Whale

The blue whale may be the largest animal ever to exist on our planet. The biggest specimen ever recorded was a 108-foot (33 meters) adult female captured by whalers in Antarctica many years ago. The carcass of this giant weighed well over 100 tons (91 metric tons). Despite their great size, blue whales became easy targets of twentieth-century hunters at sea. Today, only 8,000–14,000 of these endangered marine mammals remain.

Supersized Fish

The two biggest fish are both sharks—and unusual ones to boot. Despite their size, the 40-foot-long (12 meters) whale shark and the 30-foot-long (9 meters) basking shark eat small floating plants and animals, not huge chunks of meat. They swim with their mouths open, collecting plankton on their comblike gill rakers. When they have amassed an enormous ball of this stuff, they swallow it down.

Groups of basking sharks will often form a long line, one behind the other, as they swim. From a distance, this procession may look like a single creature—and may explain historical reports of giant sea monsters.

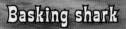
Basking shark

Whale shark

Giant Squid

The giant squid, *Architeuthis*, is the world's largest invertebrate. The record-holder is a 59.5-foot-long (18 meters) specimen that was discovered on a beach in 1878. These giants live deep in the ocean's depths, so they have seldom been seen alive. The giant squid's eyes, as large as dinner plates, are the largest of any animal's on Earth. The enormous eyes help them see the faint light emitted by fish in the inky depths of the ocean. When squid find their prey, they grab it with sucker-covered palms at the ends of their long tentacles.

In the last 50 years, several previously unknown species of giant squid have been discovered. Recently, one of these deep-sea giants attached itself to the bow of a French ship. Startled sailors were surprised to see the creature's sucker-covered tentacles covering the portholes. Perhaps occurrences such as these inspired tales of the ship-sinking kraken.

Giant Sea Serpent or Real Sea Creature?

Thirty-six-foot-long (11 meters) oarfish are the longest bony fish alive. These silver-skinned, eel-shaped "kings of the herrings" will linger near the surface when they are sick, looking much like a languid sea serpent.

FACT ATTACK!

The largest sea turtle is now extinct. Scientists named it Archelon, meaning "ancient turtle." Archelon was the size of a car and lived in the seas of what is now North America.

Speedy Fish

The streamlined shapes of certain fish are designed to slice through water like knives through butter. The fishes' sleek bodies and strong, muscular tails enable these sea creatures to reach speeds we land dwellers can only dream of.

Sailfish

Mako shark

Fast Fish

Sailfish are the world's fastest fish. They race through the water, reaching peak speeds of around 60 miles per hour (96 km/h). One sailfish was clocked at 68 miles per hour (109 km/h). Although this speed was maintained for a short distance of about 100 yards (91 meters), it is still over twelve times the speed of the best Olympic swimmer.

Mako Shark

The mako shark, which scoots at about 60 mph (96 km/h) in pursuit of live food, is a champion high jumper that can leap 15–20 feet (4.5–6 meters) into the air. To break free of the water and soar this high, the mako shark needs a "running start" of about 22 mph (35 km/h).

Bluefin tuna

Dwarf
sea horse

Atlantic flying
fish

Bluefin Tuna

Although the bluefin tuna's highest recorded speed is 44 mph (71 km/h), it is
thought to travel at short bursts of up to 64 mph (103 km/h). It is the largest
of the tunas and one of the largest bony fishes, reaching a length of 12 feet (3.6
meters) and a weight of three-quarters of a ton. The record for a bluefin stands at
1,496 pounds (679 kg)—the same weight as three full-grown gorillas!

Fish Who Fly

Because water is thicker than air, it can slow down even the strongest
swimmers. To get around this, the Atlantic flying fish will leave the water
and take to the sky. By flapping its tail and using its outspread fins like
wings, one of these 10-inch-long (25 cm) "fish out of water" can glide as
far as 300 feet (91 meters).

Slowpoke

Who's the slowest fish in the sea? Most people agree this distinction goes to
the 1.7-inch-long (4 cm) dwarf sea horse, which travels about five feet (1.5
meters) an hour. The only parts of a sea horse's body that move rapidly are
the pectoral and dorsal fins on the head and back.

Strange but True

Fish have evolved to fill nearly every possible habitat in the ocean. To do so, they've undergone many remarkable changes and acquired many odd traits—at least by our standards.

Sea horse

Four-eyed fish

Father Sea Horse

With a head like a horse, a pouch like a kangaroo, and a tail like a monkey, an adult male sea horse barely resembles a fish. But it's true: the fins, gills, and scales are firm proof that this animal is a member of the club. As strange as they may appear, sea horses act even stranger. For instance, after mating, the males become pregnant, not the females. The female sea horse places her eggs in the male's pouch. The male sea horse fertilizes the eggs and carries them inside the pouch until they hatch two to three weeks later.

Four-Eyed Fish

Do you wish you could look in two directions at the same time? The four-eyed fish can! This fish doesn't really have four eyes, but each eyeball has two sets of pupils, irises, and corneas with a thin strip of tissue between each set. The upper eyes ride above the surface of the water while the lower eyes stay below.

Archerfish

Porcupine fish

Leafy sea dragon

A leafy sea dragon easily hides in underwater gardens of seaweed.

Aquatic Sharpshooter

Archerfish squirt water to shoot down insects on branches over their heads. You could say they act like living water pistols. To shoot, the archerfish places its tongue against a groove on the roof of its mouth. This forms a tube. The fish then sticks its snout up out of the water and snaps its gills shut. This forces a jet of water through the tube and into the air. When the drops hit the target, the insect falls into the water and is quickly gobbled up.

Puffer Fish

When threatened, puffer fish gulp down water or air and inflate themselves like balloons. This makes the puffer fish hard to swallow, and most animals will leave it alone. A close relative, the porcupine fish, goes one step further. Its body is covered with sharp spines that stick straight out when this fish is fully inflated. Some kinds of puffer fish and porcupine fish have deadly toxins in their bodies—a third reason not to mess with these unusual animals.

Quiz

The answers to all these questions are somewhere in this book.

How many can you find?

If you are an invertebrate, what don't you have? (page 4)

Can you name three types of fins? (page 6)

What are gills used for? (page 8)

Why can sea creatures grow larger than land animals? (page 40)

What does it mean to be cold-blooded? (page 8)

What keeps sharks from sinking? (page 9)

What is meant by countershading? (page 25)

What sea creature has a pouch like a kangaroo and a head like a horse? (page 44)

What do crabs and lobsters have in common with spiders and ants? (page 30)

How did cleaner shrimp get their name? (page 31)

How do baleen whales eat? (page 34)

What has eight arms, a parrot's beak, and green blood? (page 28)

What sea creature may have made people believe in unicorns? (page 35)

What is the relationship between sharks and dolphins? (page 36)

What sea creature may be the largest animal to ever live on Earth? (page 40)

How do bottlenose dolphins "see" underwater? (page 37)

What animal may have inspired the novel *Moby Dick*? (page 35)

In what part of the world will you find penguins? (page 39)

Can you name two ways porcupine fish protect themselves? (page 45)

How does a sea star eat? (page 27)

What's the name of the deepest place in the ocean? (page 20)

How do clown fish help sea anemones? (page 15)

How do snapping shrimp stun their prey? (page 31)

What sea creature has eyes the size of dinner plates? (page 41)

How long can an elephant seal hold its breath? (page 36)

What fish is the fastest swimmer? (page 42)

How do archerfish get their food? (page 45)

How many do you remember?

Your Sea World

Your diorama folds two ways for your choice of colorful under-the-sea worlds. Choose your favorite backdrop to display your assembled sea creatures.

Photo Credits

Pages 4–5: Purple jellyfish / National Oceanic and Atmospheric Administration/Department of Commerce (NOAA/DC); Crab © Getty/Dorling Kindersley; Yellow tang © Jami / stock.xchng; Ray © iStockphoto.com / Paul Johnson; Seal © iStockphoto.com / Silense; Sea turtle © Getty/Image Bank; Seabird © iStockphoto.com / Nancy Nehring. Pages 6–7: Popeye catalufa © Phillip Colla Photography; Dogfish shark denticles © Dennis Kunkel / Getty Images; Close view of iridescent scales © Tim Laman / Getty Images; Growth rings © Kim Taylor / Nature Picture Library (NPL). Pages 8–9: Gills of a spotted coral grouper © Phillip Colla Photography; Shark liver illustration by Davide Bonadonna. Pages 12–13: Sculpin © Corbis; Anemone © iStockphoto.com / Steve Baines; Hermit crab © iStockphoto.com / Jasmine Grimmett; Ammonite fossil by Dlloyd / Wikipedia; Shore cling fish © Christophe Courteau / NPL. Pages 14–15: Gorgonian sea fan © iStockphoto.com / Chuck Babbitt; Moray eel © Douglas Faulkner / Corbis; Flame angelfish © Phoby / Animal Pictures Archive. Pages 16–17: Eelgrass courtesy of Rhode Island Eelgrass Mariculture Facility; Bat ray / NOAA/DC; Goby and shrimp © Mike Kelly / Getty Images; Geoducks © Justin Bookey. Pages 18–19: Ocean sunfish © Phillip Colla Photography; Salmon © Daniel J. Cox / Getty Images; Green sea turtle © Doug Perrine / NPL; Fish school © Stephen Frink / Corbis. Pages 20–21: Foraminiferans © Karl Ebleton for the Continuous Plankton Recorder Survey; Cardinal fish © Yuji Law; Anglerfish © David Shale / NPL; Viper fish and gulper eel © Doc White / NPL. Pages 22–23: Lionfish, pink stonefish, lined surgeonfish © iStockphoto.com / Dan Schmitt; Torpedo ray © Wolfgang Pölzer / Alamy. Pages 24–25: Wrasses © Keoki Stender / Fishpics Hawaii; Butterfly fish © Piednoir / AquaPress; Emperor angelfish swimming with juvenile © Fabrice Bettex / Alamy; Flatfish © Brandon D. Cole / Corbis. Pages 26–27: Coral garden, Great Barrier Reef © iStockphoto.com / Ian Scott; Lion's mane jellyfish / NOAA/DC; Giant sea star / NOAA/DC; Sand dollars © Phillip Colla Photography; Chocolate chip sea star © Wolfgang Pölzer / Alamy. Pages 28–29: Helmet-head octopus © Jeff Rotman / Getty; Squid © iStockphoto.com / Dan Schmitt; Mimic octopus as sea star © Visual&Written SL / Alamy; Mimic octopus as flounder © Brandon Cole Marine Photography / Alamy; Chambered nautilus © John White. Pages 30–31: Spider crab © iStockphoto.com / Dennis Sabo; Snapping shrimp © Images&Stories / Alamy; Dungeness crab © iStockphoto.com / boomzphoto; Coral banded shrimp © Andre Seale / Alamy. Pages 32–33: Great white shark © Jeff Rotman / NPL; Manta ray © Jeffrey L. Rotman / Corbis; Hammerhead shark © Amos Nachoum / Corbis. Pages 34–35: Beluga whale © Brian Skerry / Getty Images; Southern right whale © Armin Maywald / NPL; Sperm whale © Digital Archive Japan / Alamy; Narwhal © David Fleetham / Alamy. Pages 36–37: Elephant seal © iStockphoto.com / Eyal Nahmias; Dolphin © iStockphoto.com / Blair Howard; Sea lion © iStockphoto.com / Johnny Habell; Orca © iStockphoto.com / Seth Akan. Pages 38–39: Loggerhead turtle hatchling © Stephen Frink Collection / Alamy; Leatherback sea turtle © Getty / National Geographic; Arctic tern courtesy of Malene Thyssen, www.mtfoto,dk/malene/ Wikipedia; Penguin © Getty Images / Hoaqui; Pelican © iStockphoto.com / Ilya Genkin. Pages 40–41: Blue whale © Bios / Photo Library; Basking shark © Royalty-Free/Corbis; Whale shark © iStockphoto.com / Harald Bolten. Pages 42–43: Pacific sailfish © Jeff Rotman / Avi Klapfer / NPL; Short-fin mako shark © Richard Herrmann / Getty Images; Bluefin tuna © Visual&Written SL / Alamy; Mirrorwing flyingfish © Stephen Frink / Getty Images; Dwarf sea horse © Jeff Jeffords. Pages 44–45: Sea horse © Piednoir / AquaPress; Four-eyed fish © Phillip Colla Photography; Sea dragon © Alan Lee / stock.xchng; Porcupine fish / NOAA/DC; Archerfish © Kim Taylor / NPL.